This book is dedicated to my husband. Without your encouragement, this book wouldn't have been possible. Thank you for standing by me and supporting me in all that I do. Love you Bobby Hopper, Forever and Always!

-Rachel Myrie

Psychopaths are real. I know this all too well. You see, I strongly believe that Psychopaths aren't born they're made. They are the product of their surroundings. They learn how to be evil.

A lot of people think that psychopaths are rare and hard to find, but I can tell you that this is not the case. You see psychos are everywhere. In fact, sometimes right in front of your very eyes. I'm here to tell you they come in all shapes and sizes. A psycho could be your neighbor, your friend, or even the little old lady down the street.

By definition, a psychopath is an individual who suffers from a chronic mental disorder with abnormal or violent social behavior. Or simply someone who is mentally unstable and aggressive in nature. In short, these are people who commit evil deeds on a daily basis and have no remorse for their acts. In fact, they actually get off on the pain they inflict on others. They enjoy the suffering they cause.

You might be wondering why I am telling you this. Maybe even wondering how this is helpful. I'm telling you this because I want people to know that psychopaths are very real. They are not just crazed people you see in the movies or just fictional characters in novels either. They exist in everyday life. I know because I was born into a family of Psychopaths!

I'm going to begin this story by telling you a little bit about me. My name is Jenny Jones and I am a 32 year old woman who is married with three boys. I have long red hair and I always wear it up in a ponytail. Yes, I am in fact a plain Jane. I prefer not to wear makeup, as I feel weird when I do have it on my face. I guess it was just never for me. I was more concerned with other more important things I guess.

One such thing that I always had a passion for was writing. It was a way for me to escape my reality and put my thoughts and feelings out on paper. It was definitely a good stress reliever. I'm guessing you probably think I'm a fairly normal person who has a semi- normal life. At least that's what most people think upon meeting me. However, they don't know the truth. They don't know the horrendous torture I suffered for years.

You see there's something I haven't told you about me, and that is I was the target of a psychopathic family. Not just any family but my own flesh and blood. When I say targeted, I mean they tried to kill me. Yes, you heard me right. My own family tried to kill me.

In order to help you understand my situation better, I will start from the beginning...

I grew up in a run down trailer. It sat alongside a quiet road in Michigan that was surrounded by weeds and grass. It was a beat up white trailer with a make shift deck. The deck was half heartedly attached, almost as if it was barely hanging onto the trailer. The run down place we called home, even had tacky and outdated widows, that you had to unlatch just to open.

The trailer sat on a couple acres of land with an old barn stationed not too far from it's side. I guess it was some sort of storage barn of sorts. It was old, dirty, and cluttered with filth. Inside were remnants of leftover cages and rotting chicken feathers. Yes, it was as one might say, the property of trailer trash. A run down dump if you will.

I wasn't that old, perhaps maybe nine or ten, but I can still remember everything as if it were yesterday. But before I get into all the events that were to transpire, I'm going to tell you about my parents.

Yes, my parents. Or as I like to say....the Psychopaths.

My mother, Tammy Clay, was a violent psychopath. Not only was she physically abusive but verbally as well. I don't know if there was ever a time in her life when she wasn't this way. I tend to think that maybe when she was a child, she might have been somewhat normal.

My mother was a beautiful woman at one time. I gathered this from the many pictures she kept of herself from the many years before my birth. Her present form was nothing short of appalling. She was 60 or so pounds overweight and sported a mustache and patchy beard. Her once long thick blonde hair was now thin and stringy.

It was almost as if her evilness had manifested into her present form. Her blue eyes were narrow and almost in a perpetual leer. It was rather disturbing to witness, especially when it was directed at you.

My mother had come from an abusive home sadly. I only know this because my mother was an alcoholic. She would seize any opportunity she could to get drunk, especially whenever she felt down or depressed. Which was quite often. When she would become intoxicated she would sit us down at the table, where we would listen to her whine. Her ranting and complaining was almost always about her family.

She had one other sister who was apparently her mother's favorite. She told us numerous stories about how her mother never loved her and treated her like shit. Which was quite an odd complaint coming from her, considering this was what she did to her own daughters.

I remember one night, she let it out that her father was abusive. He like her, was an alcoholic. He abused her and her sister.

She went into a tirade about how she came home from school one day to find her father drunk and ready for a fight. She went on to tell us how she ran into her room and locked the door. She recalled how she was so scared because he was beating on the door as hard as he could. All the while she was there, she told us she had contemplated suicide.

This was something that always stayed with me. I saw her as a very broken and sad individual. This always made me pity her and believe that it wasn't her fault for her abusive behavior. At one point I actually believed she was the victim.

However, as I would learn many years later this was a manipulation tactic of hers. She used the "poor me" to make us feel sorry for her and stick around. That is until Tabitha and I discovered what she really was. When we seen her for the true monster she really was.

Tammy was weird that way. One minute she would be completely normal and then turn into a raging psychopath the next. You see my sister and I were young children who were left in her care. Sadly, we were the perfect guinea pigs for her abuse.

Now you are probably wondering where our father was through all this. Most people would wonder how someone could let their wife torture and abuse their children. This was something I asked myself for years. However, it became apparent to me in the coming years that he was no better than her. He was just as sick and twisted. He was her enabler.

My father, Jimmy Dann, was an abuser as well. He was a serial cheater, liar, criminal, and thief.

My father worked all the time. It was almost as if he used work as an excuse to get away from my mom. Quite frankly, I didn't blame him.

He and my mother had a sexless marriage. They slept in the same bed, but never had much of a sexual relationship. Yes, I know it's sad i say this. I only know this from the many drunk tirades my mother had. Sadly, all of which we were included in. Almost always against our will.

Jimmy was always out looking for women to screw. He was famous for having sex with women while he was "on the job" so to speak. He was so reckless with his sexual encounters that he actually gave Tammy a STD at one point.

Now any normal woman would have left his ass, but my mother stayed because she couldn't make it in the real world. My father knew this and took advantage of it. He knew she was weak, he had her backed in a corner. She couldn't get out and had to accept his lewd and adulterous behavior.

He was also a very well versed liar and thief. My mother caught him cheating numerous times. From sneaking out late at night to missing my birthday, so he could go out on the town to meet his next squeeze. At one point, his mistress was even calling our house and asking to speak with him.

Of course my father lied through his teeth. My mother would rage at him and even have physical fights that lasted well into the night. Only to have her take him back within a couple of days time. This was a constant cycle. My mother hated his guts as he did hers, yet they stayed together. A match made in hell by the devil himself.

For as long as Jimmy was my father, he was always fucking things up. At one point, shortly after I was born, he decided to commit grand theft auto. He stole a vehicle of some kind and tried to store it in a buddie's warehouse. Of course the cops had tracked it down and arrested them both on sight.

Not only was my father a criminal but he was violent. He abused me and my sister Tabitha to no end. We were the constant targets of his blinding raging fits he'd go into. My mother would stand by and watch with a grin plastered on her face.

He would beat us within an inch of our lives and she would just smile. That sick twisted smile she always sported.

That's when I knew something wasn't right. They were sick. They were psychopaths.

They were famous for playing the perfect parents in public and terrorizing us in private. After they would commit they're abuse, they would threaten us in any way they could. They would tell us if we told anyone what was occurring we'd get it even worse. We took their threats seriously because we couldn't imagine abuse worse than what we were already enduring. Quite frankly, the thought alone scared the hell out of us.

You see this was the way things were. Now that you know a little bit about my family, I'm going to begin my story.

Late Night Interrogations

The very first kind of torture my sister and I endured were the late night interrogations. This happened more times then I could count. It really picked up when i turned 13 or so. I guess it was because I was hitting puberty and becoming a woman so to speak. You know growing up, maturing if you will.

I think the thought of my sister and I starting to grow up scared them, and they had to put fear in us so to speak. It went something like this...

I remember coming home from middle school, my sister and I had just received our report cards. Something we dreaded. We feared getting our reports, because we knew if we didn't have near perfect grades we would be facing the interrogations. I remember quietly entering our trailer hoping Tammy wouldn't hear us. However, we didn't have that kinda luck. She was sitting on her ass, parked in front of the TV, watching some soap opera show.

"Well, how did your day go?" she asked in a low growl. All i could muster was, "It was alright."

She sat there still, glued to the TV. I walked over to the fridge to get a snack when she barked, "Well, where's your report card? I know you had to have gotten it? Where's it at?"

I hastily grabbed my report card out of my bag and gave it to her.

"Gee, thanks." she snarled as she ripped it out of my hand.

I stood there, just waiting for her reaction. I had gotten a C- in math. That kinda grade wasn't acceptable around here and warranted a beating for sure.

She was nodding her head as she went down the list of grades...and then it happened. It came to the math grade. She whipped her head around at me, got her fat ass up off the couch and came towards me.

"What the fuck is this!!" she screamed as she maniacally waved my report card around.

"I tried my hardest.." was all I could stammer.

Tammy looked at me with that evil leer and grabbed me by the hair and started dragging me over to the sink.

"Did I tell you you could talk? You little fucking bitch!" she screamed at the top of her lungs.

She pulled me up to the sink by my hair, and proceeded to force my head under the dirty sink water. I remember fighting her, trying to keep my head from being submerged all the way. But it was no use.

The harder I fought, the more she pushed me under. I was gasping for air, taking in the water, I could feel myself drowning slowly. I could hear her laughing, as I fought to get air. She suddenly let go of me and I fell backwards onto the floor. I was gasping for air like a fish out of water. My sister had ran and hid in her room. She was smart.

Tammy leaned over me and said, "Betcha you'll think twice about talking back to me, you little bitch!" she sneered as she went back to the couch. "By the way, I'm gonna show your father your grades, and tell him how you disrespected me," she said quietly, as she sat on the couch, as if nothing had happened.

I laid on the floor, trembling, soaked, and afraid. For I knew, that much worse was coming.

I quietly picked myself up off the floor and went back into my bedroom. Sure enough, Tabitha was there, hiding under the bed. We shared a bunk bed in the tiny little space we called a bedroom.

"What happened?" she asked quietly as she looked at me with concern in her eyes.

"Tammy, tried to drown me in the sink." I replied quietly.

Tabitha looked at me with a confused face. "What did you do?" she quivered.

"I simply answered a question. According to her I disrespected her." I replied as I sat down on the floor. Tabitha gave me a surprised look and crawled into her bed.

"Did you get good grades on your report card?" I asked quietly.

"Yes, all B's," she quietly answered.

Here I sat, hungry and scared. I'm not gonna lie, I was jealous that my sister was able to sleep soundly tonight. I wasn't going to be so lucky. I knew if I wanted to avoid any more abuse it was best to stay in my room.

So I too, crawled into my bed. Where I lay, trying to relax after my ordeal. The bunk bed creaked, as my sister tossed and turned beneath me. I looked out the window facing me, intently watching the sun as it began to set. I often wondered what it must be like to be a normal kid, in a normal family.

All I could remember is the feeling of being pulled out of my bunk bed and falling to the ground. I was on the top bunk by the way.

I was awoken by landing on my bedroom floor, I was crying and holding my arm. It hurt so bad.

I landed on my arm, when I was pulled from my bed. Before I could even process what was going on, I was drug across my bedroom floor and through the hallway by my hair, as Tammy was yelling and screaming at me.

"Get up you little bitch!" "Did you think you were gonna get away with it?" she screamed she continued to drag me.

I was crying and trying to get her to let go of my hair. When we reached the living room, she let go of me and I rolled over.

Jimmy was sitting on the couch looking at me. He had a weight lifting belt in one hand and a wire hanger in the other.

"So what's this I hear about your math grade?" he asked as he looked at me with a sick intent.

I stood there frozen, unable to answer. Before I knew it, Jimmy had gotten up off the couch and was coming toward me. All the while he was violently swinging his weapon of choice.

The head of the hanger had been straightened out, so that it was a straight line that had been cut to a fine point. I instinctively rose my hands to protect my face. Then I felt it. The stinging slashes that came one after the other. He relentlessly swung at me as my screams filled the room.

Tammy was standing in the corner laughing hysterically. I could feel my flesh ripping as each gash was made. The blood was running down my arms as Jimmy continued his brutal assault. I lay there on the floor screaming with tears running down my face. At that moment he stopped. Almost as if to settle himself down. His eyes were widening and he had a sick look of satisfaction smeared across his evil face.

"Teach her a lesson!" Tammy screamed from the corner as she pointed to the belt.

Jimmy looked over at the belt, as if he had forgotten he had grabbed it. I laid there in my own blood praying he would let me go to my room. He dropped the hanger on the floor and ran over to the belt. He picked it up gently, and looked at me with a look of pure evilness.

"Get your fucking ass over here," he screamed in a voice I had never heard before.

I was too weak to move and crippled by my own fear. I just laid there on the floor, looking at him with defeat in my eyes.

He saw that I wasn't going to get up. That's when he decided to take measures into his own hands. He came towards me with the intent to do severe damage.

He stood over me and started beating me with the weightlifting belt. With each blow I could feel him putting more force behind each one. With every hit, I could feel the wind being knocked out of me.

I scrambled to breathe while my mother laughed and cheered Jimmy on. He kept hitting me until he couldn't hit me anymore. I laid there like a limp noodle, just waiting for the end. Suddenly, he stopped and nudged me on the side with his foot. I guess to make sure he hadn't killed me. I was breathing but barely.

"That oughta teach ya!" he said in a loud voice. "Get your ass in your room before I lay into ya some more!" he said as he waved the belt in the air.

I could barely move and started to crawl towards my room.

"Oh my god! She's crawling? What a dramatic little bitch!" my mother screeched as she looked at Jimmy.

"You oughta beat her some more, really give her a reason to crawl" she scowled.

Jimmy chuckled as he went back to the couch, as my mother followed him to her usual spot beside him.

I continued to crawl down the little hallway to my bedroom. I tried my hardest not to look back, for fear of setting them off again. Once I reached my bedroom, I stopped crawling and laid on the floor. Thanking god they didn't kill me.

Hot Wax and Candlelight

I woke up the next day, in what seemed like a daze. It was foggy, blurry, and quite frankly weird. My arms had dried blood caked on them, along with numerous gashes. I wondered how I was going to hide this. I decided it was probably a good idea to cover them with a long sleeve shirt. I knew if my parents seen me parading around with their handy work on full display it would for sure anger them.

"Breakfast is done," Tammy screamed from the kitchen.

"If you wanna eat, you better get your asses in here," she barked as she slammed the dishes on the table.

My sister and I looked at each other and silently went to the table. Tammy was throwing the food on the plates as my father came stomping towards the table. He silently pulled out his chair and plopped down.

Tammy threw her fat ass down as hard as she could. My sister and I sat there as Tammy and Jimmy fought over the food. It was like they were in a competition to see who could snatch up the most grub. After they were done filing their plates my sister and I slowly started getting our food.

We all sat in silence as we ate. Then suddenly out of the blue, Tammy decided to say something.

"Well girls, I have some news!" she said with a smile on her face. "I'm going on a getaway with my girls and I'm leaving today," she said as she looked at us with a smile plastered on her face.

We both sat there looking shocked.

"In case you are wondering, I'm going to Las Vegas!" she exclaimed.

I was secretly rejoicing on the inside. She would be somewhere else causing havoc. That meant I wouldn't have to deal with any of her daily outbursts or verbal abuse.

We both acted like we didn't want her to leave and that we'd miss her. She ate it up, and was apparently enjoying the idea of us missing her. My father on the other hand wasn't happy she was leaving. After all, if she was gone it simply meant he actually had to do something around here. Not to mention the fact that he knew she was going to fuck around on him.

I never really understood why he got upset, when he was constantly cheating on her. I guess in his mind it was OK if he did it, but a crime if she did.

He sat there sulking, while she was beaming with happiness. Tabitha sat there looking sad and playing with her food.

"Will you bring us goodies back?" she asked quietly.

"Yeah, of course. If I have any money left." Tammy replied. "Well, I gotta get going." she said as she scarfed her food down. She hastily got up, leaving her dirty plate on the table.

For the next two hours, Tammy was busy packing all of her trashy clothes, makeup, and shoes. My parents' bedroom looked like a tornado had ripped through it. Jimmy was hastily trying to pick up all of my mom's shit that was thrown around the room. All the while he was pissing and moaning as he went along. Tammy was practically running out of the trailer as we stayed behind with dishes in our hands.

I remember going to the window to see Tammy leave. Part of me was relieved, and the other part was sad that she got to leave this hellhole. Tammy was too busy trying to stuff all her bags into the trunk of the car to notice us. She was cursing and kicking the car as she tried to fit more shit into the trunk. My father heard her loud mouth from inside the trailer and decided to give her a hand. This was something he never willingly did. I guess he was happy to send her off.

Tabitha and I spent the rest of the day picking up the multiple messes that were left behind by our mom. All the while, Jimmy sat on the couch watching TV. It seemed to be my parents' favorite past time. We were like slaves. We did all the work while they sat on their asses, stuffing their faces with junk food.

As the sun began to set, Jimmy looked at us and told us it was time for bed. And that's when I knew he was up to something. It was only 8 o'clock, that was very early for us. Too early in fact. My sister and I looked at each other in a rather confused manner. Jimmy continued to look at us in a rather irritated way.

"Well?" he barked as he stared right through us. Tabitha and I took

Tabitha and I took that as a hint to hurry ourselves to our room. We turned our backs to him and quickly walked down the little hallway that led to our room. Tabitha jumped into her bottom bunk and I climbed up into mine. We both remained quiet, for fear that Jimmy would hear us talking. We would receive some sort of beating for simply conversing.

It was the most awkward evening for us. We were laying in our bedroom, quiet as little church mouses. The TV was blaring and you could hear the Jerry Springer special word for word. I rolled over on my side, as I tried to get comfortable. The cheap bunk bead creaked and squealed under my weight. I didn't hear any movement beneath me.

Suddenly I heard it, the sound of a car pulling into our drive way. I laid still and listened quietly. I could hear my dad get up off the couch and open the trailer door as he went outside. My dad was never really sneaky around us kids. I guess he thought we were little dumbs shits that couldn't put two and two together. Of course when our mom was around it was another story.

It wasn't long before I climbed down from my bed and snuck out into the kitchen. I slowly crept up to the half open door and looked out. I could see my dad and a strange woman talking. She was tall and thin. Her hair was long, thick, and blonde. She was very beautiful and feminine. This woman was the exact opposite of my mother.

I had often wondered why he married Tammy. She didn't take care of herself and was just plain gross in appearance. She was never very feminine, something that most women just seem to have. I wasn't sure why he had children with her, simply because he was constantly cheating on her with numerous women. This was a perfect example of his many twisted hookups.

As I continued to peek at them from the door, the woman started to gently caress his arm. All the while looking into his eyes lovingly. He didn't stop her from making these intimate advances, not even once. She coyly grabbed his hand and started to lead him to the barn. He didn't hesitate, he followed like a dog chasing a bone.

I couldn't believe what I had just seen. I slowly peeked around the corner of the door, hoping to see what it was they were doing. However, they had already entered into the barn. The barn door had loudly slammed shut behind them. I stood there for a moment, trying to decide what to do.

I knew what I was going to do, but it was risky. I mustered up all the courage I could and slowly went outside. Once I got to the bottom of the deck, I did one quick scan of the yard. It was all clear and I was ready to make a break for it.

I ran as fast as I could to the side of the barn making sure to stay low to the ground. I started aiming for the nearest barn window, only to have my attention drawn to a window farther away from me. I could see a flickering light, almost like that of a candle. I slowly snuck up to the window. As I got closer I could hear the laughter of Jimmy and his mistress.

The window was clean enough for me to poke my head up and look in. That's when I seen something that I wish I hadn't. Jimmy had undressed the blonde woman and had tied her to one of the barn posts that was settled in the middle of the barn floor. She didn't resist, but rather seemed to willingly go along with his tactics.

He walked behind her and grabbed the back of her hair, pulling her head back as he caressed her nipples with his other hand. She moaned and closed her eyes as she writhed on the pole. He let go of her hair and went over to the far side of the barn, where he picked up a candle and a lighter.

He walked back over to his mistress and stood before her. He took the candle and started tracing it from her mouth down to her breasts. Circling her nipples, and then down to her sex. She let out a loud moan, almost as if she had just hit orgasm. Then he pulled the candle away and grabbed his lighter.

I watched as he lit the candle, not sure what he was going to do next. He walked over to the woman and began to put the flame on her skin, she started fighting even though she was unable to get away. I heard her yelling and screaming while he laughed maniacally. That's when he started dripping something on her.

At first I couldn't tell what it was...at least I was unsure of what it was. And then it hit me, it was burning candle wax. He stood in front of her, as he poured wax on her breasts. She was writhing in pain, screaming for him to stop. He ignored her pleas and started pouring it onto her stomach and lower regions.

It was the most disturbing thing I had ever seen in my life. She was in agony and he was getting off on her pain. I couldn't look anymore and ducked down from the barn window. I could here her screams radiating from the barn, while he was yelling at her.

I made a mad dash back to the trailer and ran back into my bedroom. I couldn't fall asleep that night. I was too disturbed by what I had just witnessed. It was then I realized my father was a sick psychopath.

Bedroom Brawl

About a week went by after that disturbing scene I had witnessed with my dad's mistress, and Tammy was on her way home. I had been dreading it just because it had actually been halfway normal around here without her.

It was late in the evening and the sun had begun to set when we heard the rumblings of her car. Tabitha and I looked at each other and then to Jimmy. He was sitting on the couch stuffing his face. Suddenly, he stopped and looked towards the driveway. He had heard the car too and knew that meant only one thing. Tammy was home.

Suddenly she burst through the door, dragging her bags of clothes behind her.

"Hi!" she yelled as she threw her stuff in the kitchen. She was stumbling around as if she was drunk. Jimmy looked at her stunned.

"Hi...how was your trip?" Jimmy asked as he stood up from the couch.

"Oh, it was wonderful!" she squealed as she turned around with a huge creepy smile plastered all over her face. And that's when it happened, when the shit hit the fan so to speak.

Jimmy walked over to her slowly, his face was in shock as his eyes drifted down to her neck.

"What the fuck is this??" he screamed as he knocked the glasses off the sink.

The sound of the glass shattering on the floor was enough to make Tabitha and I scatter to our rooms.

"Oh this ol' thing..." she said as she laughed in Jimmy's face. At this point Jimmy was boiling over with rage, his face was as red as a tomato. "Were you fucking somebody?" he screamed. As he inched closer to her face.

"Get the fuck out of my face!" Tammy screamed as she shoved him as hard as she could. Jimmy was sent backwards into the dining room table, scrambling to catch his balance. Tammy stood there smirking at him, apparently admiring her handiwork. He scrambled to his feet as he lunged towards her, pinning her against the wall.

"Were you fucking someone, you worthless whore?" he screamed as he tightened his grip around her throat.

Her face was turning red as she struggled to breathe. Her hands were searching the counter for anything that might be a weapon. Jimmy was so intent on choking her, he failed to notice this.

That's when her hands found the steak knife that had been left out. She grabbed the knife and stabbed Jimmy in the shoulder.

"That's what you get you motherfucker!" she screamed as he writhed on the floor in pain.

Tammy was standing over him with a crazy smile smeared on her face.

"You ever touch me again you motherfucker and it'll be your last!" she screamed as she stormed off into the bedroom.

We could hear Jimmy's cries from our bedroom. He was screaming and cursing us all the while enduring extreme pain. We didn't dare leave our rooms for fear we could be next. A part of me knew this wasn't over, it never was. It was always a long drawn out production. Sure enough as I had predicted, it started up again. Only this time it wasn't Tammy who started it.

Jimmy walked past our bedroom in a rage, almost as if he was on a mission. He threw open Tammy's bedroom door, and found her on her bed naked. Suddenly, we heard what seemed to be that of a struggle. The rustling of the sheets and the sound of bodies being thrown around. Then the screams of protests started.

"No!" she screamed as we heard the wall being kicked. "You pig, get the fuck off me!" she screamed at the top of her lungs.

We didn't hear any sound of Jimmy's voice, just Tammy's loud protests. Suddenly, without warning the pleas stopped and turned into loud moaning. Their fight had just taken a twist, a sick and disturbing one at that. The violent fight that had just occurred moments ago,was almost non existent now.

Instead it had turned into a sick fuckfest. I realized at that moment that something was terribly wrong with both of them. They delighted in hurting each other. They got joy out of watching each other suffer. Somehow or another, they also got off on the sick mindfuckery they performed on a daily basis.

As hard as we tried to drown their moans out, it didn't matter or seem to work. They continued long into the night, as we desperately tried to drift off to sleep. Sleep was our way of escaping our reality.

A Crazy Mistress

The sunlight was streaming into our bedroom so brightly it woke me very suddenly. I lifted my head up from my pillow and listened. I didn't hear a single sound in the house, not even in the kitchen. I looked around our room confused. Tabitha was fast asleep. I quietly got out of my bed and walked up to my bedroom door. I cautiously peered out into the hallway. It was quiet, nobody was up or moving about. Suddenly all the silence was interrupted by a loud ringing from the phone. I ran back to my bed and laid there.

The phone kept ringing. Then I heard Tammy come stomping out of her bedroom.

"Who the hell is calling us this early?" she screamed as she stomped through the house.

I could hear her knocking stuff over as she trampled through the kitchen.

"Hello?" she answered angrily. Silence followed. Then I heard her start screaming angrily into the phone. "Who the hell are you and why do you want to speak to my husband?" she yelled.

Then I heard her slam the phone down and come waltzing down the hallway.

"Girls, get your lazy asses up!" she screamed as she walked past our room. Tabitha and I got out of our beds and started to frantically clean our room.

"Jimmy...Some bitch is calling our house asking for you!" Tammy screamed as she started throwing shoes at him.

"What the fuck is wrong with you?" he asked as he jumped out of the bed and started walking down the hallway towards the kitchen.

She followed him out, demanding to know who and why the woman was calling for him. "Who the hell is she?" Tammy raged as she started shoving him.

Tabitha and I peeked out into the hallway, too afraid to come out.

"Quit fucking shoving me!" he yelled as he pushed her back.

Then the phone started to ring again. This time Jimmy answered it. "Hello," he answered quietly. "I'm sorry you got the wrong number," he said as he put the phone down.

Tammy walked over to him, "Who was that?" she yelled as she started waving her arms.

"It was some woman," he said as he started walking to the fridge.

"Don't you turn your back on me... who was that bitch? I know you've been fucking around on me!" she yelled as she started to throw glass plates at him.

Each plate was whizzing by him. They just barely missed him, as they shattered into pieces everywhere.

"Are you fucking insane?" Jimmy screamed as he ran towards the door and out to the vehicle.

Tammy was in a rage, her face blood-red, and her beady eyes were bulging from her head. She ran to the door and screamed, "Don't you come back, you motherfucker!" she yelled as she was standing at the door, looking like a white trash queen. Her robe was half closed, her hair matted to her head, and her makeup was running down her face.

She watched as Jimmy drove away. She was alone now. Granted we all knew it wouldn't last long.

Jimmy would come crawling back like the piece of shit that he was. And she would take him back because she was just as slimy. Quite frankly, they deserved each other. Somehow or another I think they both knew they were a match made in hell.

Tammy started to cry hysterically as she hung on to the open door. She slowly lowered herself to the ground and collapsed into a giant heap.

Then it happened again. The phone rang. Tammy looked up at the phone, her eyes mimicking that of a crazy persons. A disturbing gleam was beaming from her eyes.

She ran over to the phone and started yelling into it. Her voice was like a pair of fingernails on a chalkboard. It was screeching and loud. Something I wished I didn't have to hear. It was something straight out of a nightmare. One I couldn't wake up from.

And then she screamed something I'll never forget. "If you ever call me again, I will kill you!" Tammy yelled.

Tabitha and I looked at each other, scared by what we had just heard. We both knew she was psychotic and was truly capable of anything.

"Should we call the police?" Tabitha

whispered as she grabbed my arm.

"No!" I said in a shaky voice. "We are gonna stay out of her way," I said as I continued to pick up our room.

While we remained in our room, we could hear Tammy going into another one of her fits. She was pulling all the pots and pans out of the cabinets and throwing them against the walls. The whole time she was screaming like a mad woman.

Pans were bursting into the walls, knocking over anything that might have been hanging on them. Glasses were being flung off the counters and onto the floor. Shards of glass were flying through the air everywhere.

We could hear her continue to scream as she hit the walls, throwing herself into them with a loud thud. The trailer shook as she raged on.

She opened the refrigerator and started throwing all the food out onto the kitchen floor. Tammy opened the eggs and smashed them on the counter as she smeared the yolks all over the place. She started to suddenly laugh hysterically, as she dumped the pot roast all over the kitchen. By the time she had finished, anything that was in the refrigerator had ended up all over the kitchen.

The kitchen looked like a bomb had exploded in it. Suddenly she stopped screaming and laughing, and started to head towards our room.

She peered into our room and immediately grabbed Tabitha and I by our hair. She proceeded to drag us into the kitchen as we were screaming and crying.

"Clean up this mess you little ingrates!" she screamed as she threw us onto the floor that was covered in eggs and milk. "I said CLEAN the floor!" she screamed as she threw some rags at us.

We were both crying as we hastily picked up the rags and started to swish around the food and liquid. Tammy stood over us as she barked orders, like a rabid dog. I continued to try and wipe up the eggs but the cloth wouldn't pick it up.

"Mom, the rag wont soak up this stuff," I said as I looked up at her holding the rag.

Suddenly, without warning she backhanded me. My body snapped back as I hit the floor. She rushed up on me and started to kick my sides. I curled up into a ball, as I tried to protect my self. When she realized the kicking wasn't working she grabbed a skillet from the floor and started striking me all over. I started to scream as tears began running down my face. Tabitha ran over and jumped on Tammy, as she grabbed her hair and started pulling on it. "Leave her alone!" she screamed as Tammy tried to throw her off.

Tabitha held onto her hair as she used her other hand to dig into her eye. Tammy let out a scream as she flung Tabitha to the floor.

"Ahhhhh!!!! You little bitch!" she screamed as she lunged towards her.

Tabitha grabbed one of the kitchen knives and held it up to her. "Don't touch me! "she screamed as she wielded the knife.

Tammy stopped and started to back up. She realized Tabitha wasn't playing around. Suddenly there was a loud knocking at the door. I was still laying in the liquid mess that was caked on the floor. All the busted plates and glasses were surrounding me.

Tammy looked at the door, confused that someone would be at our home this early in the day. Not to mention unexpected as well.

Tabitha held onto the knife, looked at the door, and ran over to me. Tammy hastily tried to straighten herself up, food particles were mixed in with her runny makeup. She hastily went to the door and opened it. She suddenly found herself greeted by the slender, beautiful, and blonde mistress of my father.

Tammy stood there, eying her up and down. "What do you want?"

she growled.

The blonde mistress sneered at her, "I'm looking for Jimmy." she replied in a cheery voice.

"Who are you?" Tammy asked quietly.

"I'm the woman who's fucking him," she sneered.

Tammy's facial expression changed from upset to enraged. Without warning, she lunged for his mistress, grabbing handfuls of hair as they both toppled onto the deck.

The other woman was screaming and getting a few punches in on our mom. Tammy punched back a few times before taking a kick to the gut. She doubled over, letting go of the mistress. The other woman used this chance to make a getaway. She slid down the deck steps and began running to her car.

Tammy was in pain but determined to cause bodily harm to this woman. She wasn't going to let her get away with kicking her. She gathered all her strength and chased after the woman.

The other woman barely made it into her car, locking the door as she started the vehicle up. Tammy ran up to the door and began beating on her window like a madwoman. "Open this damn door!" she screamed as she picked up an over-sized rock that was in the driveway. It was like a miniature boulder and surely could cause some serious damage.

Tammy ran up to the car again and started slamming it into the window, leaving fractures and cracks in the glass. The mistress was in shock and couldn't believe what was happening. She hastily put her car in reverse and tried to back out.

My mom wasn't going to have it and chased after the car. She jumped on to the hood of the vehicle and began striking the windshield with the over-sized rock as she screamed, "You ever come back here, I will kill you! Do you understand me bitch?" she screamed as she was still hanging from the hood of the car.

It was at that moment, that the mistress knew Tammy was unstable. She hastily put the car in drive and took off. The car was jerking back in forth, as Tammy was thrown from the hood of the car. She laid in the driveway, apparently satisfied by her behavior.

Finally, she stood up and looked towards the road with a smug look on her face. From that day forward, we never heard or seen my father's mistress ever again. It was like she had disappeared from the face of the earth.

An Email Account and Transsexuals

Not too long after the incident involving Jimmy's mistress, we embarked on our never ending journey of moving. You are probably wondering what I mean by this. It is actually quite simple. Our family was very unstable. Jimmy was the only one who worked, and was our only income. Therefore, our family struggled alot. Even the simple feat of paying the bills was hard.

Tammy sat on her ass and never made any attempt to get a job and help out the family financially. Since Jimmy was manipulative, selfish, and just plain sadistic...each job he had never lasted long. So there were multiple periods of uncertainty.

We ended up moving to a slum house in a very bad area of town. Jimmy got a job in an office somewhere, managing projects, I guess.

To be completely honest, I was never quite sure what he did exactly. It was always an ever changing story.

Now the house we moved into was nothing short of a dump, a three bedroom one to be exact. The house was literally falling apart. The floor was destroyed and the cheap cabinets were barely hanging on the walls. Not to mention all the rooms were poorly heated. The backyard was barely there, patches of dirt mixed with rocks and weeds. It looked like an empty landfill, the only thing missing were the mounds of trash.

We had a somewhat make shift fence. There was only one side of fencing that separated us from our neighbors. It was a sad excuse for a fence indeed.

The only thing I was excited about was the fact that I would have my own room. It was something I had been looking forward to for a long time. Our bedrooms were on the top floor, while our parent's were on the bottom. Something Tabitha and I were thankful for. We didn't want to hear the sounds of sex that seemed to always linger in the night.

It wasn't long after we moved in that Jimmy lost his job. We didn't find out for weeks that this had happened though. He managed to hide this from Tammy for awhile. Until one day, she started to question him.

"Jimmy, where's your check?" she snarled as she stood in the kitchen glaring at him.

Jimmy was sitting at the table, scraping at his food. He didn't say anything. Tammy continued to stare at him with her beady eyes. Jimmy could feel her gaze burning into his soul.

"Well?" she snarled as she slammed down the dishes.

Still no response from him. He kept his head lowered as he stared at the table. He always behaved in this manner when he had to explain himself. I guess he figured if he ignored something or someone long enough, it would go away. In this pitiful situation that wasn't going to happen.

"Do you think I'm a fucking idiot?" she screamed as she started slamming the cabinet doors.

Jimmy got up from the table and stared at her with his dead eyes.

"I lost my job!" he screamed as he kicked his chair into the table. Tammy was furious

"How could you fucking lose your job!?" she screamed as she flew into a rage.

At this point Tabitha and I were in the living room and we both knew better then to stick around. We made a mad dash up the stairs. That's when the screaming started.

Not even a couple minutes later we heard loud booming and banging and the sound of someone being thrown up against a wall. And then it stopped....it was quiet. Suddenly, we heard the door slam. Shortly after we heard Tammy screaming uncontrollably while she sobbed.

Neither one of us dared go back downstairs for fear of catching Tammy's rage. She continued to scream and destroy the downstairs for about an hour. Then it stopped almost as suddenly as it had started.

From that point on, it was the quietest night we had ever experienced in our lives. Knowing it wouldn't last long, Tabitha and I took full advantage of it.

The sunlight of a new day came streaming in our windows and was the only thing that woke us up. We both quietly got out of bed and went downstairs.

Tammy was parked on the couch watching Jerry Springer as she greeted us with a "Good Morning". This totally caught us off guard, and we sheepishly replied "Good morning."

"After you get done with breakfast I need your help with something." Tammy said as she put Jimmy's laptop on the coffee table and looked at me.

"OK," I replied quietly. I went into the kitchen and made a bowl of cereal. I tried to drag out eating my breakfast for as long as I could. Tabitha stayed in the kitchen and looked at me wearily. Tammy was still parked on the couch. She was stuffing her face while she watched TV.

After I got done with my breakfast, I cautiously went and sat down next to Tammy and asked, "So what do you need help with?"

She quickly opened the laptop and sat it on my lap. "I want you to open Jimmy's email" she said coldly. "I know you know his password from when you had to help him sign up for his yahoo account." she said as she stared at me.

"Alright," I said quietly as I pulled up the yahoo login. I quickly put in his email and lastly his password. I was taken aback by what was coming up on the screen. I suddenly realized he had been hiding a very dark secret. My face turned pale, my palms began to sweat, and my stomach began to turn and twist. I knew if Tammy had seen this earlier, Jimmy was as good as dead. I kept trying to scroll past the disturbing emails I was seeing, only to see more.

"Well, don't just sit there, let me have the damn laptop!" she screeched.

I hurriedly handed it over to her. She sat there quiet at first, suddenly her face began reddening. She was squinting her eyes, almost as if she couldn't believe what she was seeing on the screen. Her hand was shaking as she continued to scroll through the countless emails that seemed to just pop up.

And then it happened, she broke down sobbing uncontrollably. She started shaking her head as she threw the computer back at me.

"How could he do this to me?" she wailed.

"How could he?" she screamed once more as tears were running down her face.

You are probably wondering what I had found and what she had seen that upset her so.

I always knew my father was a sadistic sicko, but this took the cake. Jimmy had apparently signed up to numerous Transsexual, Bisexual, He She, and Gay sites. Now if that wasn't bad enough he had taken his perversions to a whole new level.

He had numerous conversations with alot of gay men. All of which he had made contact with on these sights. Some of the men had emailed him naked pictures of themselves, while others simply wanted to hook up for a quickie. They had emailed him dates and times and he had replied with the times and dates he was available. It was enough to make Tammy sick .

Jimmy also had an Asian "fetish." He had subscriptions to Asian fetish sites and bondage torture sites as well.

His perversion knew no bounds. And it didn't stop there. Besides the sex sights and infidelity, he had apparently been hiding something else. And that was where the family funds were going.

According to his email account, he had dropped $800.00 dollars on a guitar. Yes, you heard me right, money that was supposed to be used for the family had been squandered for a musical instrument. It was sad and pathetic all at the same time. I was curious as to how he was going to explain all this away.

While we were struggling to put food on the table he was taking the family money and buying guitars. That thought lingered in my head for quite awhile. It was at that moment that I realized he really didn't give a damn about any of us. He only cared about his needs and wants. Apparently we were irrelevant.

Tammy sat on the couch bawling her eyes out, I sat there completely numb.

Within a couple of minutes I heard the rumbling of Jimmy's van as he pulled into the driveway. My mom sat there, tears still rolling down her face. It was very rare that Tammy was ever this nice to me. It was usually only if she wanted something, and in this case it was to get into my dad's email.

Suddenly, we heard the door open and Jimmy came parading in as if nothing had happened. He threw some 100 dollar bills down on the table and stared at Tammy.

She wiped her face and got up off the couch. Suddenly without warning, she charged Jimmy and threw him into the wall as she was screaming obscenities. Jimmy threw his arms up to block himself form her blows. Tammy continued to hit and punch whatever parts of him that were within reach.

"What the hell are you doing?" he screamed as he was hit in the gut. He doubled over onto the floor.

Tammy stood over him screaming, "You like trannies and Asians? You sick bastard!" she screamed as she continued to take out her anger on him.

"You like men too?" she yelled as she continued to try and kick him.

Jimmy dodged her kick and grabbed her by the leg, as he pulled her to the floor. She hit with a loud thud. Jimmy started to hit her in her face as he screamed, "You wanna fucking assault me you bitch?"

Tammy fought back as he continued to scream at her. Without warning he pulled a Swiss army knife out of his back pocket and put it to her throat.

"You piece of shit bitch," he screamed as he pushed the knife closer to her skin. Her skin was sticky from her sweating so much. The knife was almost gleaming as it inched closer.

Tammy stopped hitting and tried to stop his hand from putting more pressure on the knife. She knew if she gave him the opportunity he would severely injure or worse yet kill her.

"Don't you ever attack me again, or I will kill you!" he screamed as Tammy started to cry.

I stood there in shock, afraid to make a move. I knew if I made the wrong decision I could be next.

It was the first and last time I would ever see Tammy crying and begging for her life. For once she was on the receiving end of the horrific abuse. Jimmy seemed to be loving the fact that he had her in such a compromising position.

It was at this moment I seen the crazy in his eyes. I knew he was a psychopath, a deranged person with absolutely no morals or conscience. I was afraid. I knew if I didn't do something I would be next on his list.

I made a run for it. I was determined to get to the phone. Jimmy let go of Tammy and lunged for me like his very life depended on it. He grabbed both my feet and I was on the ground in a matter of seconds. I fell to the floor with a loud thud and a stinging pain on my side.

"What the hell do you think you are doing?" he screamed as he grabbed my hair and pulled my head back.

"You think you're getting the fucking phone?" he screamed as pulled my head back even farther.

I laid there crying as he continued to pull my head back farther. I was having a hard time breathing with my neck being pulled back at such an angle. Jimmy knew this and continued to pull back on me, as if his goal was to snap my neck in two.

Tammy was on the floor catching her breath, sitting there in shock. She was watching him slowly kill me. Then without warning she grabbed the knife he had tried to use on her, and raged forward at him. Jimmy turned his head only to see Tammy coming at him. He dropped me like a rag doll and dodged out of her way. I was laying on the floor trying to catch my breath. My face was red and flush, possibly even purple from the strangulation.

Tammy got back to her feet and held the knife up at him. He stood there staring at her, his eyes blazing like fire.

"Go ahead, stab me" he said under his breath. He looked at her with rage in his eyes.

"You can't make it on your own." he said under his breath. "You kill me, and who's gonna provide for you and the kids?" he sneered.

Tammy stood there, with a look of

realization on her face. She knew deep down she needed him. She needed him for everything, she depended on him. It was the ultimate checkmate in his game.

She knew he had checked her. She knew he was right. He stood there just staring at her. She dropped the knife and just looked at him with a look of disgust on her face.

Jimmy had successfully done it again. He had manipulated her to the point of no return. He had her under his thumb and he got off on it. It was rather sick to watch this transpire between them.

They were both sick, sadistic, and psychotic. The type of people that should have been locked up a long time ago. They were capable of anything, absolutely anything at all. And that's what scared Tabitha and I. They were ticking time bombs, ready to explode at even the slightest of the slight.

Jimmy walked over to the table and sat down as if nothing had ever happened. He grabbed a crescent roll off his plate and slathered it in butter.

Tammy stood there just looking at him as if he had completely gone mad. "So what the hell are we going to do, we have no money?" she yelled. "How are we gonna pay the bills?" she asked with a nasty look painted on her face.

Jimmy looked up at her as he stuffed his face full of more food.

"Well, I went and got some money from pawning my tools and shit." he said as his food rolled around in his mouth.

"I'm gonna have to get the girls' T.V.s and pawn those as well." he said as he sat there looking at her.

Tammy just looked at him in disbelief.

"Fine, do what you gotta do." she said as she stomped out of the kitchen and made her way to the bedroom.

Jimmy continued to eat his food as I lay there on the floor. I slowly got up and made my way to my bedroom where I collapsed onto the bed. I stayed there for the rest of the day.

Pawn Shops, Disconnected Utilities, and Incestuous Behavior

Within the following days my dad had begun the infamous pawning process he so dearly loved. He took our T.V.s, radio, and CDs. Basically anything he could find to pawn for a buck. This was to be a way of life until I escaped my abusers in the not so distant future. Something I could never have seen coming.

As you can imagine, this wasn't nearly enough to pay our rent or bills, it was only a temporary solution to an ongoing problem. So within the next couple of months we had managed to have our water and electricity both shut off. It was hell, a hell I can't even begin to describe. We went a week or so without water.

Our bathroom stunk of piss and feces. Everyone was taking turns relieving themselves and not flushing, in an attempt to conserve what little water we had.

We had no shower or bath water. So in order to avoid smelling of sweat and stink, we used bottled water from the store to wash with. It was the most demeaning thing I had ever had to do in my life.

If that wasn't bad enough we couldn't even afford to wash our clothes and dry them. As an end result, my sister and I had to wear dirty clothes to school for days on end. We would attempt to wash them the best we could with bottled water and soap in the bath tub. After we would finish we would try and hand ring them out to the best of our ability. Then we would lay them out on a chair in the kitchen overnight in hopes they would be dry by morning.

I can't begin to tell you the amount of

times we would wake up and our clothes were still wet. It was terribly uncomfortable having to slide on wet pants or even shirts, and let our body heat dry them. Not to mention that musty wet smell they seemed to harbor.

As the years passed, this became all too common. We were constantly moving from one slum rental to the next. By the time my parents had finished, I had attended three different high schools. I managed to stay at one particular school for two years, even though my sister and I didn't quite fit in.

After I graduated it seemed as if

Tammy and Jimmy finally found a somewhat permanent residence. This new home that I would live at for two years was the beginning of the end for me. I had no idea that within two years my life would change drastically.

Now you are probably wondering where Tabitha has been through all this. You see up until this point I had been the child that took the brunt of the abuse. Tabitha had merely stayed under the radar for the majority of the time. That too would change almost immediately.

I can't pinpoint what started it exactly

other than the fact that Tabitha had become just like Tammy. Not to mention, Jimmy had taken a very sick interest in his own daughter. So disturbing in nature, that Tammy had even begun to take notice. She started to call him out on his incestuous tendencies every time there was an inappropriate episode.

I remember the very first incident quite clearly. To be honest I wish it was something I had never heard or had to bear witness to. It all started rather randomly actually. It was right after we had moved into our new rental home that sat on a side road. That road lead straight out to a highway. A very busy one at that. So busy we heard the sounds of traffic late into the night.

Jimmy had been sitting in his reclining chair, that sat in the living room right across from Tammy. Of course she had her ass parked on the couch intently watching T.V. Jimmy would every now and then glance at the T.V and then back at Tammy, almost as if to see if she was looking at him.

Suddenly Tabitha, who was wearing short shorts and a skimpy tank top, came walking into the living room. She stood there watching the T.V, almost as if trying to find the right moment to muster up enough courage to ask Tammy something.

Then it happened, Jimmy sat there just staring intently at Tabitha. His eyes went to her legs and slowly moved up to her breasts. He kept staring, hardly blinking, as he acted on his sick urges.

"What the hell are you doing?" Tammy yelled as she sat staring at Jimmy with a look of pure shock.

"I'm not doing anything!" he yelled back at her with a look of surprise on his face.

"You sick fuck!" she screamed as she got up from the couch and made her way over to him.

"Now you check out your daughter???" she yelled as she waved her hands in the air at him.

He got out of his chair and stood

over her. "I didn't do no such thing...you are one sick bitch!" he yelled as he stormed out of the house. Tammy went running after him as she continued to yell obscenities at him.

Tabitha stood there in shock. We both looked at each other with a look of confusion on our faces.

Suddenly, we heard the breezeway door slam shut and in came waltzing Tammy. She came charging right up to Tabitha with rage in her eyes.

"You little fucking whore!" she screamed as she started shoving Tabitha towards the living room chair. I made a a clean getaway, fearing for my own well being.

Tammy kept shoving Tabitha until she had knocked her into the chair. It was all over for my sister at this point, she was cornered and vulnerable. Tammy went into a rage where she began punching and kicking Tabitha as hard as she could. Tabitha was screaming and crying, all the while she was trying to block the blows. This went on for a while.

I had contemplated calling the cops but had remembered what had happened last time I tried to do that. I knew that it would be all over for me if I indeed did try to call for help. And so went this vicious cycle. A part of me knew that none of this was normal or right. However, I was too immobilized by my own fear to try and put a stop to it.

I was 19 and had no car, no job, or anywhere to go even if I did make my escape. That was what held me and my sister back from simply packing up our stuff and leaving in the middle of the night.

I think deep down my parents knew this. It's why they abused us in the sinister way that they did. We were their punching bags, always there to take a beating and never fight back. It was the sick truth sadly. We were prisoners to psychopaths. Psychopaths who were capable of anything and willing to do anything to silence us.

Later on that evening, Jimmy came back to the house and of course Tammy acted like nothing had ever happened. She had resumed her place on the couch and was watching T.V intently.

Jimmy quietly walked through the dining room and into his room. He closed the door quietly behind him as Tammy sat there motionless.

About an hour or so had passed and I had made my way into the little area that was my makeshift room. I jumped into my little bed and got cozy and started to drift off to sleep. Within what seemed like hours, I was awoken by a loud screaming match that was taking place in my parents bedroom. I opened my eyes halfway, the house was somewhat lit and blurry. I wondered if I was in a dream or if I was simply imagining this.

Suddenly the door burst open and Jimmy was practically running through the dining room as Tammy ran behind him wielding my sister's underwear in her hand. Jimmy made it to the kitchen, desperately seeking some sort of weapon to defend himself with. Within minutes, Tammy had jumped him and was beating the shit out of him with her bare hands.

"You sick bastard! What the hell is wrong with you?" she screamed as she continued to hit him. He was opening the kitchen drawers desperately searching for something with one hand while he tried to fend her off with the other.

"Here, you sure you don't want to masturbate with your daughter's underwear some more?" Tammy screamed through clenched teeth.

She continued to hit him anywhere she could. Jimmy finally gave up trying to find a weapon and turned around to face his attacker.

She hit him in the chest with a clenched fist while trying to rub the soiled undergarments in his face. He started swinging his arms radically in every direction in hopes of clocking her.

However, all his attempts to fend her off were pointless. She came at him like a rabid dog, relentless and looking to bite.

"Tammy!" he screamed as he kept trying to fend her off.

"Tammy, stop!" he screamed. "Stop it already you fucking psycho!" he screamed.

Tammy threw the underwear at him, while she stood there staring at him with hate and disgust in her eyes.

Acne and Disfigurement

And so it began, this cycle between the both of them. Tammy catching Jimmy making inappropriate advances on his own daughter. It was sick and depraved to say the least. Sadly, instead of Tammy leaving Jimmy, and removing us from his toxic and disturbing behavior she chose a much different path. She chose to stay and take her anger out on my sister and I. After all, she knew she had nowhere to go. She had no job, income, or savings. She was stuck living with this sicko she called her husband.

Jimmy seemed to revel in the idea that he could make sexually inappropriate advances on his own daughters and nothing would be done.

After the initial fight that broke out between them over the underwear masturbation incident, Tammy channeled that rage into trying to disfigure Tabitha and I. Tabitha unfortunately got the brunt of the physical abuse.

You might be wondering what exactly I mean by disfiguring. In fact, it was something so simple yet insidious. Something a normal person wouldn't have even thought to do. You see Tammy had a way of masking her abuse.

The abuse came in a form of trying to help with a very common adolescent problem. That problem was none other than acne.

You see, we both were well into our teenage years and like every other teen had started to develop acne.

Tammy had started to become insanely jealous of us due to her husband's disgusting behavior. Initially, it would only occur after she would catch Jimmy committing a perverted act or eying Tabitha. But then it progressed to simply doing it just to inflict pain.

I'll never forget the first time she decided to go after Tabitha. It was late one evening, after a family dinner, and Jimmy had once again been caught checking out his own daughter.

They exchanged some words and he angrily took off to bed. I had started to clear off the table while Tabitha sat there picking at her food. Tammy eyed her up and down with an evil intent.

Tammy slammed down her silverware and looked at Tabitha as she muttered, "Get over here."

Tabitha looked up at her from her plate slightly confused.

"Did you not hear me?" she asked coldly. "Get your ass over here now!" Tammy growled.

Tabitha got up from her spot and walked over to Tammy. Tammy got up from the chair and motioned to it. From that moment on it was all over and I think Tabitha knew it.

She sat down in the chair as Tammy ripped off her shirt and started to dig into her back with all her might. Tabitha started to cry and desperately tried to get away from her.

"What are you doing?" she screamed. "Stop, you are hurting me!" she cried as she tried to get away from Tammy.

"Hold still you little bitch!" Tammy screamed. "Or I'm gonna make it worse!" she said as she dug her nails into her skin.

Blood started to drip and the skin was being ripped open. Tabitha continued to cry as she tried to push Tammy's hands off her. Tammy had this disgusting grin smeared on her face as she inflicted more pain.

Without warning, Tammy grabbed Tabitha's head and slammed it against the table.

"You wanna fight me some more?" she yelled loudly. "I'll fuck you up so bad you'll wish you were never born!" She yelled as she ripped her head backwards and held it there.

"I can't breathe..." Tabitha gasped as her head kept being pulled back.

At this point I couldn't take it anymore and came rushing at Tammy.

"Let her go!" I screamed as I jumped on her. This took her completely off guard and she let go of Tabitha's hair as she fell back onto the floor. I ran over to my sister to make sure she was OK. Her nose was bleeding from having her head smacked onto the table and her back looked horrendous.

Then it happened, without warning I took a blow to the back. I doubled over onto the floor. Tammy grabbed me by my hair and pulled me up to the chair. I kept fighting her, my arms flying, trying to come in contact with her. I was hoping she would let me go but it was of no use.

She slammed my head onto the table and held me there while she took her other hand and dug her nails into my back as hard as she could. All I can remember is the excruciating pain I felt. It was as if a knife was being drug through my skin. All the while she was doing this, she let out a cackling laugh. She was getting some kind of sick pleasure out of causing us pain. I remember crying and fighting. Eventually I just gave up and laid against the table. The pain was so great that I eventually got to the point where my skin had become numb. I had become numb to her nails ripping my flesh like it was paper.

Tabitha was in the corner crying and shaking. This was our life. We lived with a demented bitch for a mother. Without warning, Tammy stopped what she was doing and let go of my hair. She stood there laughing at us. Her face contorted into a macabre expression.

She kicked the chair out from underneath me and yelled, "Get your ass up and go to your rooms! You pathetic pieces of shit!" she screamed as she glared at both of us.

I could barely move at that point and started to crawl towards the living room.

"What do you not understand me?" she said in a eerie tone. "Get your asses up and go to your rooms!"

I slowly picked myself up from the floor, Tabitha ran over to me and helped me up. She was crying and shaking much like I was.

"You better go to your rooms before I change my mind!" Tammy yelled as she started throwing all the dining ware off the table and onto the floor. She was in another one of her violent rages yet again.

We scattered off to our rooms as quickly as we could, without looking back. We could hear her yell behind us, "Next time it will be your faces!"

To our horror, those last words she yelled where not a threat but a promise.

That was the most sickening part about all this. She was that disturbed and driven by her own sick jealousy of her daughters, that she was willing to commit the most heinous of acts on us.

You see her zit popping escapades became more frequent and sometimes weren't even driven by her husbands lewd acts. It became something she liked to do just to inflict pain. It was her hobby so to speak.

Tammy had gotten to the point where her marriage had become sexless, so to speak. Quite frankly, I can't say I didn't see it coming. Jimmy had lost all interest

interest in having sex with her. To him she had become repulsive so to speak. Instead he spent most of his time viewing porn on-line. His porn obsession had started to take over what little bit of a life he had.

Tammy knew what he was doing, and she didn't bother to confront him or fight with him over it. It was as if she simply didn't care anymore. After all she got her sexual pleasure from inflicting physical pain on her daughters. She was a special kind of sick in my eyes. She was a far more dangerous psychopath then Jimmy ever could be.

What made her more dangerous was the fact that she would stoop to any low to cause physical harm. After all inflicting pain was like a drug to her. A high if you will.

Not only was she extremely violent, but when she would go into her rages she simply seen red. I don't know what exactly was wrong with her, but it was like she wasn't in her body. It was as if something took her body over completely. Almost as if a demon jumped inside her and made her do all the sadistic things she did. It was a very disturbing thing to witness.

As you can probably guess, more of

her abusive episodes were to occur. It just so happened that not even a week later my sister and I were to be her victims once again. Only this time I was first.

Fight or Flight

I remember it quite vividly, it was late one evening and Jimmy had gone to bed early so he could masturbate in peace.

I had begun to clean the table off and started the dish water for the dishes. Once the sink was filled completely, I had started to submerge all the dishes in the sink as I looked out the kitchen window. Not even ten minutes had passed before Tammy had strolled into the kitchen. I kept doing the dishes with my back to her as if I hadn't noticed she was there.

She walked up behind me and grabbed me by the back of my shirt. She started to drag me back to the kitchen table. I tried to hold on to the kitchen counter in hopes of not arriving at the dreaded kitchen chair.

"Let go of that damn counter top," she yelled as she made a fist and started pounding on my shoulder.

I let out a scream as I held on tighter and tried to pull myself up to the sink.

"Let go!" she shrieked again as she

hit my shoulder with another blow.

That was the hit that took my arm off the counter top. I fell down onto the kitchen floor grasping my shoulder as I sobbed loudly in agony. Without mercy my mother struck again. Before I knew what was happening, she grabbed for my injured arm and pulled it back behind me. I started screaming and trying to escape from her.

She twisted my arm even harder as she let out a twisted laugh. "You wanna fight me you little bitch?" she yelled as she twisted my arm yet again.

I was in so much pain, tears running

down my face, as I laid there. She started to drag my limp body over to the kitchen table by my injured arm. It was like that of a rag-doll, unresponsive and limp. All I could think to myself was that one day this would all be over, just not right now.

Tammy continued to try and drag me but my body was too heavy and I couldn't find the strength to move. She was getting irritated and enraged that I wouldn't cooperate with her violent demands.

"Get the fuck up!" she screamed as her face turned beat red. She was standing over me. I could feel her eyes burning a hole into my soul. I laid there, looking at the walls. I had no desire to move, no desire to follow her demands.

"Get up! Get up!" she started screaming continuously as she started to kick my limp body.

I curled up into a fetal position and took each kick, as I waited for it to be over. As with each of her violent tantrums, almost all came to a sudden end.

As each kick came rolling in, I began to realize that this rage wasn't going to end until she got what she wanted. She continued to scream like a mad woman since she wasn't getting her way.

It wasn't long before Jimmy came storming out into the dining room from his chambers.

I laid there on the floor, with a bloody nose, and possibly a broken arm. Even though it was still functional, I didn't want her to know that.

"What the fuck is going on?" Jimmy asked as he was rubbing his eyes.

"I'm trying to get some sleep, I've got work tomorrow!" he growled as he stared at Tammy.

"I'm trying to get this bitch to sit in the chair." Tammy yelled back at him.

"Oh for fuck's sake, are you serious?" Jimmy asked as he had a look of confusion on his face.

"Really, this fucking late at night?" he asked as he crossed his arms over his chest.

"Yes! this little bitch is gonna learn a lesson. Sitting here disrespecting me when I tell her to do something!" she yelled as she grabbed the table cloth off the table.

Jimmy just stood there looking at her in disbelief. I kept waiting for him to stop her, to help me. I kept waiting for him to finally stand up to her. To finally put her in her rightful place. Sadly it didn't happen, instead he did the unthinkable.

"Where do you want her?" he asked as he walked up to me and grabbed me around the waist.

Tammy stood there with an evil grin on her face, and an evil intent within.

"Put her on the chair while I tie her to it with this table cloth," she said as she glared at me.

He reluctantly picked me up and sat me on the chair, holding me tightly as she took the table cloth and tied it around my wrists. After she was done with that, she proceeded to run it through the back of the chair and knot it.

I was panicking, I knew this was the end. I wasn't going to make it out alive. The only way I was going to leave this house was in a body bag.

I could see it in her eyes, this wasn't just torture anymore. She had lost it and apparently my screams weren't enough to sustain her sick appetite. Her ultimate goal was my death.

She had always been a psychopath but she was upping her game so to speak. Now she was crossing over into being a murderer. A murderer who was out for blood and tears. I was to be her first victim and probably not her last.

I sat in the chair, face covered in sweat beads, as I looked over at Jimmy. He looked at me with his empty eyes and went back into the bedroom. He closed the door behind him loudly.

He was my only chance. My only chance for escape. Tabitha was sleeping in her room. Even if she had been up, I don't think she would have ventured into the kitchen for fear of being next. All my options were exhausted. I had nothing left to choose from. Tammy knew it, and she was enjoying this moment.

She stood there for a moment simply staring at me with those evil eyes.

"You know no ones gonna help you." she snickered as she walked into the kitchen and started opening the drawers.

"No one is gonna come save you now!" she said a little louder as she slammed one drawer closed.

"You know, if you would've listened to me and not fought... this could've been over already?" she said as she continued to dig through the drawers. She kept moving down the kitchen counters, desperately searching for her weapon of choice. As she was boom banging around in the other room, I heard some movement coming from Tabitha's room.

I looked over at Tammy, her back towards me, as she continued on her mad search.

I turned back to face the living room, scanning it for a sign. Then my eyes met Tabitha. She was on all fours peaking around the corner at me. A look of confusion and fear was smeared all over her face.

I frantically scanned the room for any

thing that could help me get out of the tablecloth handcuffs I was wrapped up in. Suddenly, I found what I was in desperate need of. It was a large steak knife that had fallen off the table when Tammy ripped the table cloth off. It wasn't far from where Tabitha was.

I looked over at Tabitha and made a motion towards the knife. For a minute she didn't quite understand what I was wanting. I once again motioned towards the knife as I looked back at Tammy.

Tammy was still busy foraging for her weapon in the kitchen. Tabitha stood up halfway and made a quick sprint towards the knife, as she kept her eyes on Tammy. She grabbed the knife and quickly made her way to me and started to cut away at the table cloth handcuffs.

Within minutes she had me free, and handed me the knife.

"Here's your chance," she whispered quietly. "You have to get out of here, she's gonna kill you." Tabitha whispered with tears running down her face.

At that very moment, Tammy had stopped digging through the drawers and held up a metal skewer. Her eyes were gleaming with pure satisfaction as she looked at her weapon of choice. Then she turned her gaze to me. I looked around trying to find Tabitha. She was gone, nowhere to be found. Tabitha had taken off so quickly and quietly that I didn't even notice.

I was still sitting there on the chair with the knife behind my back. My mind was racing, I only had one chance at my getaway. I had to make this move count if I wanted to see the light of day again.

The only thing that was going to possibly get me out of this situation was going to be the element of surprise.

Tammy had no idea that Tabitha had freed me or the fact that I also had a weapon. A weapon I wasn't going to hesitate to use.

Tammy started to walk over to me casually and she was twirling the skewer around in front of her. Almost as if she was trying to put more fear into me, if that was even possible.

I sat there still as a rock. My eyes were dilated and I was hardly blinking. My mind was racing. It was playing out every possible scenario that could take place in the next moment.

Tammy stood in front of me, her eyes were in a perpetual glare. She didn't even look human at this point, but more like an evil demon. Her eyes were now black as the blackest night. It was as if she was soulless.

"Since you want to fight me," she said under her breath. "I'm gonna put you through hell!" she growled as she gripped the skewer tighter.

"Instead of using my nails to dig into your back, I figured we could dig out any acne with this skewer!" she said as she cackled loudly.

This was my moment. The only time I could catch her off guard. I had to act as soon as possible, before she realized I wasn't her hostage anymore.

She stood there laughing so hard she was almost doubled over. She was getting so much sick enjoyment from the thought of being able to mutilate her own daughter. It made my stomach turn as I sat there watching her. I was simply waiting for the right moment to spring into action. Then it happened, I had an opening and I went for it.

Without hesitation, I jumped up out of the chair and charged Tammy. She was still laughing uncontrollably until my body made contact with hers. It was like I was playing football and I had just made my first tackle. I had a surge of adrenaline rushing through my body.

Before Tammy came crashing down on the ground her face had a look of pure shock sprawled on it. Her hand had let go of the skewer as she was sent backwards onto the ground. I braced myself for the impact as I tucked my head to the side. When we came crashing down, Tammy's body hit with a loud thud. Then my body came slamming into hers. She let out a loud grunt of pain.

She instinctively tried to grapple with me in an attempt to get me off her. She hadn't realized I had a knife in one of my hands. That's when I made contact with her. I made a decision to go after her leg.

Without hesitation I plunged the knife into her calf, hoping to stop her from being able to run after me.

She let out a loud scream and began

to grab her leg. I pulled the knife out and went for the other leg. I was going to make sure she wasn't going to be able to get up. She kept screaming and trying to push me off of her.

I was going to plunge the knife into her leg once more but realized I had her where I wanted her. I clutched the knife in my hand and made my getaway.

I scrambled to my feet and started running through the kitchen, making a mad dash to the breezeway door. I could hear Tammy screaming and shrieking behind me. I didn't dare look back. I knew if she kept screaming she was going to wake Jimmy up and I'd have him to contend with. I reached the door, opened it and ran through the breezeway. I came to the back door that led outside onto the road. My hands were shaking so bad, that the doorknob was almost impossible to open.

Suddenly, I jiggled the doorknob open and started to run through the yard. My heart was beating through my chest, as I continued to hear muffled screams coming from the house. Sweat was streaming down my face and body as I continued to run towards the street. I took one last look behind me. Nothing, no one was coming after me that I could see. I wasn't going to stop running though. I knew there was a chance Jimmy would come bursting out of the back door.

I turned around to face the road only to come face to face with a passing car. The car hit their brakes as I tried to stop myself from running into them. I came slamming into the side of a Grey Dodge Durango.

I looked back once again at the house, almost out of breath, and then my heart sank. Jimmy had come running out of the back door yelling at me.

I looked back at the driver and started to yell.

"Please, let me in!" I screamed as I tried to jiggle the car handle. The driver hastily unlocked the car door and opened it for me. I jumped in and locked the door as I yelled, "Go, Go, Go!"

The man who was behind the wheel stepped on the gas and suddenly we were off. I looked back at the hell hole I called home and seen Jimmy run up to the road. He stopped and stood there as he watched us drive away into the night.

I let out a sigh of relief as I sunk back into the car seat. The leather interior was soft and surprisingly inviting. For once in my life I felt like I could relax. I sat there with my eyes closed as the car drove down the main highway.

A More than Helpful Stranger

Within minutes I opened my eyes and looked over at the driver. He was a tall man with dark hair and a thick beard. He seemed to be a medium build and somewhat athletic from what I could tell.

"So do you want to tell me what that was all about?" he asked in a worried tone as he looked over at me for the first time.

I sat there looking at the floor feeling somewhat uncomfortable and embarrassed at the same time.

"They tried to murder me." I said in a low tone as I looked back at the road.

"What???" he asked as he continued to stare at the road. His eyes were squinting in the darkness as he was trying to watch the oncoming traffic.

I sat there, quiet as a church mouse, in the passenger seat. I didn't want to repeat myself, let alone relive the incident. I quickly looked over at him. He was still staring at the road as he flipped on his turn signal. It was at that moment I realized we were pulling into a gas station.

It was lit up like a Christmas tree, the lights were so strong they were blinding. It was eerily empty for a gas station on a main highway.

The driver drove past the pumps and pulled up directly in front of the entrance. He parked the car and turned it off abruptly. He looked over at me suddenly with a look of concern on his face.

"What you just said back there....that really happened?" he asked in an inquisitive tone. He continued to stare at me until I answered.

"Yeah...they tried to kill me." I answered as I looked over at him with tears running down my face.

"Listen I can take you to the police station, you can file a report," he said as he grabbed my hand.

"No!' I said loudly. "No, I just need to find a place to stay for the night." I said under my breath.

"You can stay with me," the driver said as he continued to look at me for some sort of response.

I looked over at him slightly confused. "You would do that for me?" I asked.

"Yeah, of course." he exclaimed as he was looking around the gas station. "My name is Matt, in case you were wondering." he said with a chuckle.

I looked at him with a smile on my face and smeared mascara under my eyes.

"Yeah, I was gonna ask...Kinda weird I'm sitting in a complete stranger's car at a gas station." I stated quietly.

Matt looked at me with a grin on his face. "Well, it's OK. I'm not like a psycho killer ya know!" he exclaimed.

"Shit...I hope not." I said as I shook with laughter.

He sat back in the driver's seat and put his head back on the headrest as he stared at the gas station entrance.

"Well, do you want anything while we are here?" he asked as he glanced over at me.

"No thanks." I replied quickly. The lights from the station were bouncing off of the store windows. They were so bright they were starting to hurt my eyes.

"Alright then, we are gonna go home." Matt exclaimed as he sat up in the drivers seat. He put the car in reverse and pulled out of the station and back onto the highway.

As we were driving, I noticed we were heading towards the north side of town. An area I was not familiar with. After all, it was the ghetto area of the city. As we drove further into the area, I started to see more people out on the streets. Some of the folks were homeless it seemed. They were wrapped up in newspapers, as they slept on the sidewalks under the city lights. Others were wandering aimlessly around town, almost as if they were looking for their next fix.

Trash and overflowing dumpsters lined the streets and surrounded the below average homes. The closer we got to Matt's home the worse it got. I was starting to get worried. I began to wonder if I had made the right decision to go along with him. It was as if I was going from bad to worse.

Before I knew it, we came up to an apartment complex that sat adjacent to the road. The whole complex was lit up, and the tenants were standing outside conversing with each other. Some of the people yelled and threw stuff at us as we drove by. Matt seemed unphased, almost as if he was used to this kind of behavior.

"Does this always happen?" I asked as I looked over at him with a shocked look on my face.

He chuckled slightly as he continued to look to the road. "Yeah, it's the ghetto." he said with a smirk.

I sat there with a somewhat confused look on my face. It was odd to me that someone could be so nonchalant about all this.

"What can I say I've lived in this area

of town for at least 7 years. You just get used to it." he said as he pulled into a group of apartments that sat at the very back of the complex.

The apartments all looked the same. They were a nasty muddy orange color and looked like they were straight out of the inner city housing areas.

"This is where you live?" I asked as I looked around. Some of the tenants were outside smoking and staring at us like we were aliens.

"Yup, this is it. Not much really, but it's my home." he said as he turned the vehicle off and unlocked the doors.

Matt got out of the Durango and started

to head up to his apartment. Within minutes, he stopped and looked back as he realized I hadn't left the vehicle. I sat there for a moment as I looked at my new surroundings. I was unsure and scared at the same time. I looked back over at Matt as he motioned for me to follow him.

"Well... you coming?" he yelled as he looked back at me.

I hastily jumped out and slammed the vehicle door behind me. I didn't have any baggage to unload, all I had was the clothing on my back. It was the weirdest feeling I had ever felt. I was starting all over again and I had not even a penny to my name.

I ran up to Matt and hastily followed him

up the flight of stairs that led to his apartment. By the time I had reached the front door, he had already unlocked it and had proceeded inside. The door was left wide open revealing a very compact living space. I stood there for a second as I looked in amazement at the tiny space he called home.

I closed the door behind me as I walked into the apartment and looked around. Matt was standing by one of the black leather couches he had crammed into a corner.

"Well, you wanna a quick tour of your new home?" he asked in an eager tone.

"Sure." I replied as I stood there.

Matt made his way from the couches

and towards what appeared to be the kitchen.

"Here is the kitchen." he said as he motioned to it.

The kitchen was very tiny and compact. There was only a small space available for the dining table. Next to the table was a small walkway that led to the dishwasher and sink.

As I walked past the sink, I came across the oven. It was boxed into the corner of the room by the trash can. Across from the oven was the washer and dryer. Which was surrounded by a good amount of wall cabinets. It was the smallest kitchen I had ever seen.

I quickly walked out of the kitchen and followed Matt over to the hallway. It was connected to the only bedroom in the apartment. We then took a couple more steps down the hallway only to come face to face with a tiny bathroom. I cautiously peeked in and was shocked at how tiny and crammed the bathroom was. There was barely enough room in there for two people. I turned back to Matt with a surprised look on my face.

He stood there looking at me somewhat amused. "What? Never seen a bathroom that small?" he chuckled.

"Honestly, no." I replied quietly as I started to walk back into the living room. I went over to the black leather couches and sat down. Matt walked over and sat down next to me.

I looked over at him only to find him looking back at me.

"I just want to say thank you...for helping me out like this." I said as I looked him straight in the eyes.

He continued to look back at me as he put my hand in his. A feeling of warmth came over me and I grasped his hand back.

"It's gonna be OK...you are safe now." he said as he continued to hold my hand. "No one is gonna hurt you anymore." he said quietly.

It was at that moment that I realized I was finally free from my abusers. I was free to live my life and be prosperous. I would no longer have to endure nights of endless torture or psychological warfare. I was finally going to be able to live a normal life. Or at least that's what I thought. I had no idea that this was only the beginning of a sick and sinister plot to finish what they had started. A plot to silence me for good...

Lightning Source UK Ltd.
Milton Keynes UK
UKRC031905170322
400250UK00003B/58